Taco Dude

By The Camacho Family

Taco Dude

By The Camacho Family

Illustrated by Anthony Camacho

Dedicated to my
family
&
Everbody that
loves Tacos!!

Taco Dude always starts with a song

Taco Dude
is a cool Dude!!

Taco Dude
is a surf Dude!!

Taco Dude
is a good friend

Taco Dude
SHREDS!!

Taco Dude
is a good sharer

Taco Dude
is a world class dancer

Taco Dude
is a beach Dude!!

Taco Dude
is a Ski Dude

Taco Dude
is a Dude's Dude!!

Taco Dude
is a reading Dude!!

Taco Dude
blades on the weekends

Taco Dude loves his family

Taco Dude
has a sensitive side

Taco Dude
hates litter bugs!!!

Taco Dude is down with recycling

Stressed out Taco Dude goes to a

Dude Ranch

Whooaa, Dude

Taco Dude
  is a two thumbs up kind
of Dude!!

Yeah Dude!!!

Taco Dude
Has lots of friends

Senior Cactus

Benny El Sol

Burrito Bro

Tico the Horse

Which is your favorite Taco Dude?

Taco Dude always ends with a song

Made in the USA
Middletown, DE
15 April 2017